T

MW00905769

Great Play, Morgan!

Illustrations by Bill Slavin

First Novels

The New Series

Formac Publishing Company Limited
Halifax, Nova Scotia

Formac Publishing Company Limited acknowledges the support
of the Cultural Affairs Section, Nova Scotia Department of
Tourism and Culture. We acknowledge the financial support of
the Government of Canada through the Book Publishing Industry
Development Program (BPIDP) for our publishing activities.

We acknowledge the support of the Canada Council for the Arts
for our publishing program.

National Library of Canada Cataloguing in Publication Data

Staunton, Ted

Great Play, Morgan
  (First novels. The new series)

ISBN 0-88780-536-1 (pbk.) — ISBN 0-88780-537-X (bound)
I. Slavin, Bill. II. Title. III. Series.
PS8587.T334G66 2001   jC813'.54   C2001-900199-1
PZ7.S8076Gre 2001

Formac Publishing
Company Limited
5502 Atlantic Street
Halifax, NS B3H 1G4

Distributed in the United States by:
Orca Book Publishers
P.O. Box 468 Custer, WA
U.S.A. 98240-0468

Distributed in the U.K. by
Roundabout Books (a division of
Roundhouse Publishing Ltd.)
31 Oakdale Glen, Harrogate,
N. Yorkshire, HG1 2JY

Printed and bound in Canada

Table of Contents

1
Soccer Genius

"Impossible! Impossible!
Land it on the rail! Five-Oh!
Go! NOOOOOO!"

Charlie wipes out his board
again. Charlie has so many
sports trophies it looks like he
won the Olympics, but hey,
you can't be good at
everything. I'm better at
skateboarding. Well, not
skateboarding skateboarding. I
stink at that. What we're
doing is video game
skateboarding.

I'm a pro at that. It's better
anyway — you can eat while

you're playing.

Charlie hands me the
controller. As I start my turn,
he says, "Did you decide
about soccer yet?"

Oh yeah. Soccer. Charlie
wants me to sign up with him.
His dad will be coaching the
team. "Hang on," I say. I'm
reverse grinding along the
edge of a skyscraper roof.
Right, right, left, down, down,

hold on, up, up, upupUP. My
fingers are flying. I'm flying.
I can do anything. How hard
can kicking a ball be, compared
to this? Plus Charlie says they
have freezies and snacks after
every game.

"Sure," I say, "I'm gonna
sign up."

"Great," says Charlie.

"Wonderful!" says my
mom, looking into the family
room. I face plant into a
dumpster. I have three
thousand points and a new
sport.

* * *

After supper, I dig a ball out
of the garage and go over to
the schoolyard. I figure I'd
better try soccer while no

one's around. I've never really played it because I don't like to run that much. But who knows? Maybe I'm a soccer genius.

Or maybe not. My first kick blops along the ground. The second one, I miss, The third one connects. The ball takes off and rattles the fence. Oh, yeah! I shake my fists and do a little jump. My winning goal will be like that.

"Whutcha doin?" a voice asks. I jump again. Aldeen Hummel, the Godzilla of Grade Three, is standing behind me. Where the heck did she come from?

"Um," I say, "playing soccer."

Aldeen squinches up her

eyes behind her smudgy
glasses. Her witchy hair
bounces.

"You should try it," I say,
just to say something.

She puts her hands on her
hips. "What for?"

Aldeen always makes me nervous, and when I get nervous, I blab. I tell her all the stuff Charlie told me: the uniform you get, how everybody comes to watch and how you get a trophy after the tournament, plus the snacks and freezies.

"You should try it," I say.

Aldeen grunts and shuffles off. I figure I'm lucky. Sometimes when Aldeen gets bored she belts you. But I'm wrong about luck. And about being bored. When I go out for first practice, Aldeen Hummel is standing by the soccer balls.

2
Tired Pizza

Charlie's dad, Mr. Lucas, starts the practice. He calls off our names and gives us our uniforms.

The uniforms are excellent: black socks, shorts, and gold jerseys that say Jim's Pizza. Perfect, I think. Most kids pull on the shirts.

Aldeen holds hers as if it's real gold. It's weird. I've never seen her like anything before. Then she sees the numbers on the back. She looks at hers. She comes over to me.

"What's your number?" she growls.

"Fifteen," I show her.

"Nah," she says. She looks around. She marches over to Bobby, a kid from our class, and says something. Bobby shakes his head. It's a mistake. Aldeen steps on his foot. Bobby howls and jumps. That's when I see Aldeen has on spiked soccer shoes — they're really old and way too big. She says something else. Bobby trades jerseys with her. By the end of practice she's traded twice more and two other kids are limping.

By the end of practice, I'm limping too. It's not thanks to Aldeen the Mean, either. I haven't run this much since ...

well ... ever. I feel as if I've been squished into cream cheese by a bulldozer. I sit down on the ground.

"Nice effort, Morgan," Mr. Lucas calls.

"Thank you." I can't move. I can't even move when my dad asks if I want a yogurt cone, You know I'm really tired when that happens.

"Way to go, Morg," Charlie says as he walks by. He's a little red in the face but he's allowed, Charlie probably ran twice as far and twice as fast as anyone else. The only kid who even came close was Aldeen. She didn't run as far though. Aldeen runs over people instead of around them. Kids are peering at

bruises under their shin pads. Others stumble past rubbing their elbowed stomachs and knuckled arms.

"Where the heck did she come from?" someone groans. I sit and stare at the ground until a pair of monster-sized soccer shoes gets in the way. I look up. Aldeen is looking down at me. Her glasses are all steamed.

"Good thing you told me about this," she says.

3
Popsicle Cleats and Spaghetti Legs

The next morning I wear my new jersey. I hurt all over, even my arms, so it's hard to put it on. My legs don't bend anymore, either. I walk to school like Frankenstein.

At school I see different coloured jerseys everywhere. I guess there were lots of practices last night. A-1 Hardware, I read. Brown's Towing. Valumarkets. Charlie walks into class and high-fives me. He's wearing his jersey too. Cool. Bobby comes in. He's wearing his jersey. Diane has hers. Will's wearing his.

"Wow!" says Mrs. Ross, our teacher. "You're all together. That's great."

It is, too. I puff up a little. I've never been on a team before.

Then Aldeen clumps in, She's a gold and purple popsicle stick, wearing her jersey over sweatpants. She's clumping because she's also wearing her monster cleats. Bobby tucks his feet under his chair. Diane rubs her arm. Will ducks.

"Aldeen, Fantastic!" Mrs. Ross gushes. Hummel the Bummel snorks something back into her nose. "Morgan said I should sign up."

Bobby, Diane, Will, and Charlie look at me. I look out the window.

After school, Charlie wants to practice.

"I'll show you some stuff," he says. He does, too, except I can't do it. Charlie zooms: I thud. Charlie shoots. I flub. Charlie dives; I trip. Charlie zig-zags. I get spaghetti legs. Plus, I still hurt all over.

"You're getting it," Charlie says.

No I'm not. I'm panting too hard to say it, though.

It's embarrassing.

"I think I got a blister on my foot," I lie.

"It's your shoes," Charlie says, "Don't worry. When you

get cleats you'll be tons better."

"Tons." I pretend to agree. For the next three days I say my foot's too sore to play. I get twelve thousand points ramping off the CN tower. Why can't you play soccer with your fingers?

4
Easy Freezies

The day before our first game I get my cleats. Maybe Charlie was right; I do feel better in them. Besides, my legs can bend again. Mom and Dad drive me to the game. They have lawn chairs and large coffees.

"Go get 'em, tiger," Dad calls as I trot out for warmups. He's pretty pumped. Hey, I'm pretty pumped.

Mr. Lucas makes us do stretches. Then Diane goes in goal and we take shots. My kick goes toward the net. Now

I'm really pumped.

The game starts. I'm on defense. We're playing Herman's Plumbing. They have red sweaters. From the opening kick, it's about two seconds until Charlie gets the ball, takes it all the way down the field, and scores.

"Yaaay."

I look over to the sidelines. All the moms and dads on our side of the centre are cheering. Somebody clangs a bell. Charlie trots back, slapping hands. Cool, I think, and we start again, only now we're winning.

Nobody scores for a long time after that. We have freezies at halftime. Mostly I watch, even when I'm on the field. Somehow, the ball always seems to come down the other side and Mr. Lucas has told us to stay in our positions.

When I'm not on, I sit near the freezies cooler, because there's some left over. Mr. Lucas yells a lot. So do the other parents. I wonder if I should tell him it all sounds the same out there. Before I can, Aldeen flattens a Herman's Plumbing player, then trips over her giant cleats. The whistle doesn't blow. The ball squirts free. Charlie takes it and scores again.

"Yaaay."

This time there's muttering with the cheers.

"Ouch!"

"Who is that kid?"

"You don't know Aldeen Hummel? Hoo, boy. Quite a family. There's the mom down there. Nobody knows where the dad is."

I look. Off by herself, there's another Aldeen, a little taller, with grey in her witchy hair and a cigarette drooping from her lips. As I watch, my mom goes over and says something to her.

"Morgan. go on for Kaely," says Mr. Lucas.

"*Kaely*!" I trot around, then Herman's finally kicks the ball down my side. It's my big chance. Kick to Charlie, I think. I wind up and boot the ball straight out of bounds.

The whistle sounds. Game over. Parents cheer.

"Great play, Morgan!" My mom is jumping up and down beside Mrs. Hummel, who's not. We line up to shake hands and someone knuckles me in the back.

"We won," Aldeen says. She's smiling. I'm smiling. Freezies, I think, then a large yogurt cone. I like soccer after all.

5
The Trouble with Hummel

We lose our next six games. Charlie's great, but nobody else is. Mr. Lucas tells us to play our positions but mostly everyone follows the ball around like a swarm of bees. I play my position: ball chasing is too tiring. Of course, that's all I do. I'm too slow for offense. On defense, one fake and I'm Morgan the Human Pretzel. Sometimes I get a good kick, but the rest are jellyfish floaters. All in all, I stink.

Aldeen isn't any better. Oh,

she can run like crazy. Dad
says she can kick like a horse.

"Exactly," Diane says,
when she hears. "Her shoes
are big enough for one."

See, the problem is, when
Aldeen runs, she flattens
people. When she kicks, it
isn't always the ball. It hurts
too, boy. We know, because it
doesn't matter who has it.
And when Aldeen isn't
whacking us, she's setting a
world record for penalties. We
lose three games by penalty
kicks.

Kids are getting grumpy.
Parents complain to Mr. Lucas
at practice.

"Everybody's learning," he
says. "Let's just get out there
and have fun."

Then he yells, "Spread out, you guys!" because the swarm of bees is starting up again, and "Careful, Aldeen!" because she's about to sail into the middle of it. I'm watching from my part of the field, where nothing ever happens. I hope she doesn't cream anybody. Bobby's already said it's my fault, because I got her on the team.

"Ish naw my fawl!" I'd said back. (My mouth was full of freezie.) And it isn't. I just told Aldeen what Charlie told me. Just the same, I wish she wouldn't sit beside me every time we're off. And I wish my mom wouldn't talk to her mom every game. Nobody else does.

FWEEEEET! Mr. Lucas is blowing his whistle, calling us all in.

"Okay, You guys, time for shooting drill." He looks us over. "Let's see now ... Morgan! It's your turn in net."

6
A New Goal

"Net?" I say. I can't believe it. "Not goalie, please not goalie."

"Yup. You haven't had a turn yet, have you?"

Darn right I haven't had a turn. I don't want one, either. All those balls shooting at you: it's scary just thinking about it. I don't say that, though. I just take the gloves from Kaely.

Everybody lines up for a kick. At me. The net feels about the size of a barn. I feel about the size of a barenaked ant. Ian winds up as if he's going to kick to the moon, and runs at the ball. I close my eyes. I'm forgetting one thing — we've also lost six games because we can't shoot worth a darn. I hear a whump. I peek and see the ball dribbing toward me. I scoop it up for my first save.

Bobby kicks, Diane kicks, Stephanie kicks, Will kicks: bloop, bloop, scribble, and bong, off the goal post. Okay, so Charlie nails one into the corner and Aldeen kicks one right over the net. It's still almost a shutout.

"I think we've got a new goalie," Mr. Lucas says. I think he's right — until just before the next game.

"I don't want to," I complain, as my dad helps me pull on the goalie shirt. The other team has a guy who shoots like Charlie.

"Don't worry," Charlie says, as Mr. Lucas tightens the gloves. "I won't let him get a shot. I promise."

Charlie keeps his promise. The rest of them shoot even worse than we do. I think it helps that everybody we play is so scared of Aldeen that they don't want to touch the ball. It also helps that Charlie gets two goals. We win. Playing goal is a breeze.

We win the next game, too. Charlie keeps everyone away, but it's my shutout. I'm a star and I don't even have to run.

After the game Dad gets me a large yogurt cone. "Great playing, Morgan," he says.

Next morning, when Charlie calls up and says, "Wanta practice?" I say, "I can't I don't want to mess up my streak."

Hey, when you're hot, you're hot.

7
Duck Shot

There's two games left before
the tournament playoffs. Mr.
Lucas says we have to win
one of them to get in. The
games are against the two best
teams in our division.

"I'll play both ends,"
Charlie says. 'They won't
even get a shot, I promise."

"Are you gonna be on all
the time?" I ask. I'm chicken
all over again.

Charlie shrugs, "It doesn't
have to be a shutout. We'll
score too."

The first game is against

Holton's Flowers. Every kid is nine feet tall. I watch them warm up. They shoot like cannons.

"Don't forget," I warn Charlie. Then I go over to Aldeen. "Aldeen?" I say, "No penalties, okay?"

She stops cracking her knuckles and looks at me. She doesn't say anything. I creep away to get my goalie sweater. There's no point getting killed before the game.

Holton's Flowers are awesome. They even have plays. It takes all we've got just to keep them from shooting. Everybody tries hard, but Charlie is amazing. He stops rushes, blocks shots, forces kids wide, kicks out of bounds. Finally, late in the second half, he steals a pass and streaks for the other end.

Everyone races after him, screaming. I'm screaming. Charlie kicks, but it's weak. Their goalie scoops it up, runs out and booms a kick back and suddenly the biggest Flower of all is coming right at me, I look upfield. Charlie has run out of gas. The only kid between me and megadoom is Aldeen Hummel.

"Get him!" I yell.

So she does. You can hear the crunch all the way around the field. The whistle shrieks. Parents roar, When the FLOWER can stand up again, he rockets the penalty kick at

my head. I duck; they score.
We lose.

* * *

"You said you'd play both
ends," I complain to Charlie
after it's over.

"Hey," Charlie says, still
red from running, "At least I
didn't duck."

"Well, this wasn't my idea,
it was yours. I stink at soccer!"

"So try practising," Charlie
says, then he turns to Aldeen.
"And why don't you try
cutting out stupid fouls so we
don't blow it?" I've never
seen him mad before.

Aldeen glares back. "I only
did it 'cause Fat Boy yelled
me to. And if you don't like

it, tough noogies. It's Morgan's fault. He told me to play."

"What?" I shout. "It is not my fault"

"Like stink, Who cares anyway? I quit."

"Oh yeah? Well, so do I." And I quit too.

8
It's Not My Fault

There's a problem with quitting: I think it makes Charlie hate me. I'm not sure because I'm scared to call him up and find out.

There's another problem with quitting. It means I have to tell my parents.

"But what about the team?" my dad says. "There's already kids away. If you quit there might not be enough players."

Talk about unfair. Now I feel even worse. I don't give in, though.

I say, "That's not my fault.

Let Aldeen not quit, then. Anyway, I stink."

"No you don't," Mom says. "You're learning. You're doing a great job in nets."

"I am not. It's just nobody gets a shot on me."

"So you're making the team play better," says Dad. "That's the idea, isn't it?"

Whoah. I like that. I mean, it's okay to think it's Charlie's fault I joined soccer, but I'd rather think the good stuff is thanks to me. Not him.

"That's right," says Mom. "And you should keep on doing it because you know who really needs some help? Aldeen does."

Now, wait a minute. "It's not my fault Aldeen wrecks

everything," I shout.

Dad sighs. "Morgan, the fouls aren't your fault. But you know what? You are responsible for her playing soccer, and that's good."

"No way! Everybody — "

"Never mind what they say," Mom interrupts. "Soccer is the best thing that ever happened to Aldeen. Her mom says she loves it and she's glad you told her. Aldeen admires you, Morgan."

Oh, yuck. This is the grossest thing I've ever heard.

"That's not my fault." I stare at my folks.

Dad says, "Nobody's talking about faults. We're talking about responsibility. You have to decide whether

you owe something to Aldeen
and the team."

"It's not my fault," I say
again. And again. And again, I
say it going outside, I say it
sitting in my tree fort, I say it
on my bike as I ride slowly
over to Aldeen's.

9
Bare Feet and Bony Knees

Aldeen lives in a little crumbly house with scraggly grass and prickle bushes that look just like her hair. I've been there once before. When I ride up she's sitting on the steps, picking at a scab on her bony knee.

"Hi," I say.

"Shut up," she says. "My mom's sleeping. She's on midnights this week."

"Oh," I say.

"Shut up."

Sheesh. I don't even want to be here, and now I can't talk.

"I don't think you should quit soccer," I whisper.

"I don't care what you think," Aldeen yells, loud enough to rattle the windows.

"SSSSSSH!" Now I'm doing it. This is weird, boy. I just want to get out of here.

I say, quickly, "Okay, but the team needs you. If you quit there's not enough players."

"That's not my fault." Aldeen wiggles her bare toes. Its the first time I've seen her without her cleats since soccer started.

"But you said you'd play!"

"I did play." Her eyes squinch up. "Didn't I?"

"But — "

"It's not my fault, Morgan.

So just get lost."

I'm starting to get mad. I can tell whose fault she thinks it is.

"No sweat," I say, hopping on my bike. It's easier to talk tough to Aldeen when you can make a quick getaway.

"Sorr-ry, Aldeen. You're right. I never should have yelled for my teammate to help me. It's all my fault. Like usual. Thanks a bunch."

Then I burn off, before she belts me.

10
Great Play

I've blown it. All I can do is show up early for the last game.

Charlie and his dad are there already. For once, I don't say anything. Charlie never says much, but he grins. Bobby arrives, then Kaely, Ian, Stephanie, Diane, Will. Parents set out their chairs. We warm up. The other team is ready. The ref is ready. We're a player short for our big game with Uneeda Taxi and it's my fault. Great play, Morgan; try not to look at anybody.

Then a car clunks into the parking lot. Aldeen piles out, running. She's got her cleats on. "I'm goalie," she yells.

"Huh?" I'm already at the net.

"I'm goalie." She's pulling the goalie shirt back over my head. I stumble, and she yanks it free. I tug my Jim's jersey back down, I don't like people seeing my belly jiggle.

"Hey, what's the big idea?"

"I play goal. You can't make me get penalties." Her head pops out of the shirt. "Gimme the gloves."

Aldeen is good: faster than me and not chicken. She even makes saves. She has to, because I'm on defense. Charlie works on scoring. He

gets a goal. So does Uneeda
Taxi. We're playing like
crazy, but they're good and
we have no subs. Still, it
could be way worse, and at
least Aldeen can't cream
anybody. I think goal even
makes her happy. Now, at
halftime, she's even talking to
Uneeda kids who go to our
school.

We start the last half. Boy,
are we tired. All we can do is
keep the ball midfield. And
then there's a mixup. The ball
is loose and a Uneeda kid is
bombing downfield. I'm back,
ready and waiting. The kid
fakes, dodges, and I'm
Morgan the Pretzel Boy again.
She sails by.

That's when Aldeen runs up

the crease and hollers, "Remember!"

The kid takes one look and drops like a stone. The ball rolls to Aldeen, who scoops it up and boots it with her monster cleats. It's up, up. And coming down. At me. Oh no. I close my eyes and scrooch my shoulders and whonk, something smacks my head. When I open my eyes the ball is bouncing to Charlie, who's wide open. He takes it down and passes to Diane. She scores.

And that's it for Uneeda Taxi. We hang on to win. We're in the playoffs. Everybody cheers. Charlie and Diane have goals, I have an assist and a sore head. My

mom hugs Mrs. Hummel. Aldeen jabs me in the arm. "You know last game?" she says. "I shouldn't have whacked that guy."

I can't believe it. The Queen of Mean saying she was wrong? Is it thanks to me? Did she believe me when I said it was my fault? Did I set a good example? Geez, maybe I am responsible.

"Yeah," Aldeen says, "I shoulda done this before."

"What?"

She shrugs. "I was tired, so at halftime I told those guys the next one to shoot would get their face rearranged after the game. Did you see that doofus bail when I yelled 'Remember?' Now I don't even have to play goal any more."

I look at her. Aldeen Hummel is smiling again. I decide to keep my mouth shut. You can't be responsible for everything.

More new novels in the *New First Novels Series:*

Robyn's Best Idea

Hazel Hutchins
Illustrated by Yvonne Cathcart

Robyn is befriended by a stray cat that's hanging around outside her apartment building but she can't give it a home because of the "no-pets" rule. She wonders why it is that most people in her class, especially Jessica Johnson, can have pets and new toys and anything they want, but she and her Mom have to make do. Still, she can come up with some good ideas.

Jan's Awesome Party

Monica Hughes
Illustrated by Carlos Freire

Jan and Sarah are trying to figure out how to spend the $40 they were given as a reward for finding Patch. They settle on throwing a party for their class -- a totally awesome party. It's all set to go except they have to have permission from the scary new principal.

Carrie's Camping Adventure

Lesley Choyce

Illustrated by Mark Thurman

Carrie convinces her Mom to take her, her brother and their two best friends on their first-ever camping trip. When they get the campsite in the provincial park their misadventures begin when they find they have forgotten to pack their food. The kids are left alone for the rest of the day to put up the tent and light a campfire and stay out of mischief.

Formac Publishing Company Limited
5502 Atlantic Street, Halifax, Nova Scotia B3H 1G4
Orders: 1-800-565-1975 Fax: (902) 425-0166